# Disney
# My First Stories

# WINNIE THE POOH FINDS FRIENDS

One morning, Pooh visits Roo's house. "Roo, would you like to **play** with me today?" he asks.

"I can't," says Roo. "I've got so many things to do."

Pooh frowns. "Nobody can play with me today. All my friends are busy."

"I'm sorry," Roo replies.
"Perhaps you can make a **new friend**."

"How do I go about doing a thing such as that?" asks Pooh. He thinks, thinks, thinks... And as he thinks, he starts to wander.

Pooh wanders and finds Piglet collecting haycorns.

"How do you make a **new friend**?" Pooh asks.

"You must be kind and reassuring," says Piglet.

Pooh keeps wandering and finds Tigger.

"How do you make a **new friend**?" Pooh asks.

"You've gotta **bounce** with 'em!" says Tigger.

Pooh keeps wandering and finds Eeyore.

"How do you make a **new friend**?" Pooh asks.

Eeyore shrugs. "Don't know, never tried. If I wait around long enough, a friend usually comes to me."

Pooh keeps wandering and thinking hard.

Along the way, he sees a young hedgehog balancing on top of a log.

"What a cheery, **playful** little fellow," Pooh says to himself.

As Pooh passes a sweet-smelling bush, his tummy rumbles.

"Excuse me!" he calls to the hedgehog. "Would you **care to share** a snack?"

The hedgehog walks right up to Pooh. **"Thank you,"** he says. "I'm pretty hungry, and those berries look tasty."

"My name is Renny," says the hedgehog. "What's yours?"

"I'm Winnie the Pooh. But you can call me Pooh. You know, Renny, I agree. These berries are tasty, but they would be even better with **honey**."

Renny perks up. "Come with me!" he cries. "I passed right by a honey tree. I'll show you where it is."

Pooh sighs happily as he licks the honey off one paw and pops a berry into his mouth with the other. "Now these berries taste **just right**."

After he finishes the sticky treat, Pooh thanks Renny. The **two new friends** sit quietly in the forest.

In the distance, Pooh sees his old friends Roo, Piglet, Tigger and Eeyore.

"Pooh, we've come to play with you!" they shout happily.

"Wonderful!" Pooh says. "We can all play with my **new friend** Renny!"

# AUTUMN
## PUBLISHING

Published in 2021
Published in the UK by Autumn Publishing
An imprint of Igloo Books Ltd
Cottage Farm, NN6 0BJ, UK
Owned by Bonnier Books
Sveavägen 56, Stockholm, Sweden
www.igloobooks.com

*Winnie the Pooh is based on the "Winnie the Pooh"
works by A.A. Milne and E.H. Shepard.*

1221 001
2 4 6 8 10 9 7 5 3 1
ISBN 978-1-80108-111-5
Printed and manufactured in China